HOT DOG BOB

and the Dangerously Dizzy Attack of the Hypno Hamsters

BY **L. Bob Rovetch**   ILLUSTRATED BY **Dave Whamond**

chronicle books·san francisco

Book design by Mary Beth Fiorentino.
Typeset in Clarendon and Agenda.
The illustrations in this book were rendered in ink,
watercolor washes and Prismacolor.
Manufactured in China.

Library of Congress Cataloging-in-Publication Data
Rovetch, Lissa.
Hot Dog and Bob and the dangerously dizzy attack of the hypno
hamsters : adventure #3 / by L. Bob Rovetch ; illustrated by Dave Whamond.
p. cm.
Summary: Having hidden the lunchbox in which the superhero Hot
Dog from the planet Dogzalot always arrives on Earth, fifth-grader Bob
and his best friend Clementine must stand alone against an evil alien
who plans to hypnotise humans into thinking they are hamsters.
ISBN-13: 978-0-8118-5601-0 (library edition)
ISBN-10: 0-8118-5601-1 (library edition)
ISBN-13: 978-0-8118-5602-7 (pbk.)
ISBN-10: 0-8118-5602-X (pbk.)
[1. Hypnotism—Fiction. 2. Hamsters—Fiction. 3. Frankfurters—Fiction.
4. Extraterrestrial beings—Fiction. 5. Schools—Fiction. 6. Humorous stories.]
I. Whamond, Dave, ill. II. Title.
PZ7.R784Hor 2007
[Fic]—dc22
2006014857

Distributed in Canada by Raincoast Books
9050 Shaughnessy Street, Vancouver, British Columbia V6P 6E5

10 9 8 7 6 5 4 3 2 1

Chronicle Books LLC
680 Second Street, San Francisco, California 94107

www.chroniclekids.com

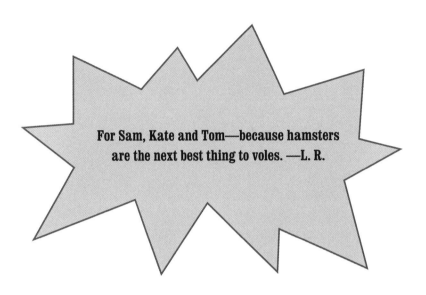

For Sam, Kate and Tom—because hamsters
are the next best thing to voles. —L. R.

Contents

Chapter 1

17 Days

I'm Bob, and I miss my old life! In my old life
I only worried about regular little stuff, like
keeping my annoying brother out of my room
and passing the spelling tests I forgot to study for.
In my old life I never even thought about
getting erased by little pencil people or
escaping from prisons made out of cheese.

But ever since a superhero hot dog popped
out of my lunch box, called me partner, and told
me we were gonna save the world from evil
space aliens, I switched to worrying about
big stuff. And I mean *really* big stuff!

"What are you doing with that calendar?"
I asked Clementine at recess.

"I'm trying to figure out when the next alien invasion will occur," she answered.

Clementine and I are best friends. We're also the only ones who have any memory of Hot Dog and the freaky aliens who keep "visiting" us here at Lugenheimer Elementary.

"Would you quit worrying about it?" I said, trying to be the cool one. "All that crazy stuff is over with!"

"Be realistic!" said Clementine. "Hot Dog said he'd be back after the Cheese Face attack, and he was. Hot Dog said he'd be back after the

pencil-people attack, and he *will* be! You have to admit it, Bob. Hot Dog always seems to know when trouble's coming."

"Heads up, Bobby Boy!" Marco yelled, passing me a football.

"I'll play in a minute!" I said, kicking it back.

"So," Clementine said, putting her last X on the calendar, "it was exactly two months and two days between the first and second attacks. And if my calculations are correct, Hot Dog should be showing up for the next big battle in exactly seventeen days. I just think we should be prepared is all."

"Okay," I said. "You prepare our superpower anti-alien attack-proof suits, and I'll go get our invisible jet boat–rocket ship out of the garage!"

"You can joke about it all you want," said Clementine, "but when the next batch of alien freakazoids decides to take over Lugenheimer Elementary and we're not ready, nobody's going to be laughing. Especially you!"

Chapter 2

What Lunch Box?

I thought all day and night about what
Clementine said. If her calendar calculations
were correct and another alien invasion
really *was* going to happen in 17 days, maybe
we *should* do something. The one thing
I knew for sure was that we were definitely
on our own. If we tried to warn our parents or
the police or anyone, they'd just think we
had overactive imaginations or tell us to stop
eating so much sugar.

The next morning I hid my lunch box
under the big bag of Chomper's dog food in
the cupboard below our kitchen sink.

"Why are you smelling the dog food?" asked my strange little brother, Bug.

"None of your beeswax," I answered politely.

"I want to smell it, too!" he said, squeezing next to me under the sink.

"Why do you always have to copy everything I do?" I asked him. "If I said the dog food was yummy, would you eat it?"

"Good idea!" Bug said, picking up a piece of Chomper's kibble.

Here's what I was thinking: Hot Dog only shows up in my lunch box, so if there's no lunch box, there won't be any Hot Dog. And if there isn't any Hot Dog, there won't be any aliens. Looking back on it, I see how stupid that sounds, but right then it made perfect sense.

"Hmm," said my mom. "Have you seen your lunch box, Sweetie? I can't find it anywhere!"

"That's okay," I said. "I'm fine with a paper bag."

"But your lunch box keeps everything so nice and fresh," said my mom. "I just can't imagine where it could be!"

Later that day in the lunchroom, Marco said, "Hey! Where's your lunch box?"

"Who cares?" I answered.

"But, dude," said Marco. "You've had that same lunch box since first grade!"

"So?" I said, wishing he'd get off the subject.

"So I miss it!" he said. "I seriously miss that lunch box!"

"You are so weird!" I laughed.

Clementine took a huge bite of her disgusting sandwich creation and mumbled, "So really, Bob, where *is* your lunch box?"

"Oh! Hey, Clem!" I said. "I just remembered we have to go work on that, um, incredibly important science project *right now!*"

"What are you talking about?" she said, taking another huge bite. "That thing's not due till Friday."

I gave her an uncomfortable look that meant, "Would you please just get off the lunch-box subject and play along with me here?" Luckily, Clementine got the hint.

"Oh!" she said. "You mean *that* science project! You're right; we'd better go work on it pronto! Hate to dine and dash, Marco. See you in class."

"Since when have you guys gotten so excited about doing homework?" asked Marco.

I wanted to tell him the truth and say, "Since a couple of months ago, when the all-mighty ruler of the planet Dogzalot (otherwise known as the Big Bun) decided to beam a flying weenie into my lunch box and make me his alien-fighting Earth partner!" But I didn't.

"Okay, what's going on?" Clementine whispered on our way out of the lunchroom.

When I told her what I'd done to my lunch box, she just laughed at me.

"I thought you were the one who said we didn't have anything to worry about!"

"I guess your calendar thing kind of got to me," I confessed. "I mean, maybe we *should* be doing something to protect ourselves."

"Maybe," said Clementine. "But what?"

Chapter 3

Rejects

When the end-of-lunch bell rang, my class went to the library for Career Day. First up was Lupi's mom, who told us some fairly good stories about her job as a firefighter. Next was Marco's kind-of-annoying dentist dad, who thought flossing was the most exciting invention known to humankind.

"My, my! What fascinating careers!" said our librarian, Miss Toenail. "All right, Angelina, it's your turn to introduce your mother."

"Um, okay," Angelina said. "This is my mom, and she, uh, works in a toy factory."

"Thank you, Angelina," said Miss Toenail.

Angelina's mother plopped a big box down on the table. It had tons of tape and the word "Rejects" stamped all over it.

"Hey, Bob the Slob and Clementine Porcupine!" yelled my least favorite person ever (otherwise

known as Barfalot). "Look, a box chalk full of rejects—just like you!"

"Yeah!" laughed Barfalot's brainless body-guard brothers, Pigburt and Slugburt. "Cause there's rejects in that box, and you guys are rejects, too! Get it?"

"Wow! You guys are *sooo* clever!" Clementine smiled sweetly while rolling her eyes.

"Quiet, everybody," said Miss Toenail, "so we can find out what's inside the box."

"Howdy, boys and girls, and thank y'all for invitin' me here today!" Angelina's mom said all excitedly. "I am *so very* lucky to work at a toy factory! It is a real fun job! I am in charge of makin' sure that all the toys comin' off the assembly line are one hundred percent perfect! But I'm gonna let you boys and girls in on a little secret. Once in a while some of our toys just aren't right. They're just a bitsy bit defective. Can anyone tell me what the word *defective* means?"

"That's easy!" shouted Barfalot. *"Defective* is what Bob and Clementine are!"

"Yeah! Get it?" Pigburt and Slugburt laughed even though there's no way they knew what *defective* meant.

"Uh, well, maybe I'll just tell y'all," said

Angelina's mother. *"Defective* is when for one reason or another somethin' is wrong with our toys. And since we at Bloppo International sell only the very most perfectly perfect toys, we always destroy our defective rejects."

"Yeah! Rejects *should* be destroyed!" Barfalot said, looking straight over at Clementine and me.

"Yeah!" Pigburt and Slugburt repeated as usual.

The Terrible Triplets were jerks to everyone, but lately they'd totally had it out for Clementine and me.

"*Shhh!*" Miss Toenail said, putting her finger up to her mouth librarian style.

"As I was sayin'," Angelina's mother went on, "for some strange reason the toys in this box

came out with a whole *bunch* of defects. And my boss said that since they were so—uh—*different,* it would be all right if I gave them to you nice little boys and girls. So, well, here y'all go. There's a Happy Hamster in this here box for each and every one of you!"

Barfalot, Pigburt and Slugburt ran up to the box and grabbed a bunch of Happy Hamsters.

"Calm down, children," said Miss Toenail. "Let's all take turns!"

But nobody was taking turns. Even Marybell Marshall, the most polite person in my whole class, was pushing and shoving to get to the box. It was like those Happy Hamsters had some kind of special magnetic power. Angelina's mother was right. These toys really *were* different!

Chapter 4

Happy Happy Hamsters

"All righty then!" said Miss Toenail. "Would everyone please say thank you to all these nice parents for helping us out with Career Day?"

Unfortunately for Miss Toenail, the kids were paying even less attention to her than usual. Nobody said thank you. Nobody said anything at all. They all just sat there staring blankly at their Happy Hamster toys.

"Oh, I am just *so* embarrassed!" Miss Toenail told the Career Day parents as they left the library. "It looks like we're going to have to have ourselves a little talk about manners!"

Clementine and I checked out our Happy Hamsters and saw that their big, bulging eyes were lighting up and spinning around in psychedelic swirly yellow circles.

"Whoa! These things are awesome!" I said.

"I guess," said Clementine. "Only mine's making me feel sort of carsick."

"Now that you mention it," I said, "I *am* starting to feel kind of dizzy."

Clementine and I might have been feeling a little bit funny, but by the looks on our classmates' faces, they were feeling downright out of this world!

"That's strange," said Clementine. "It's almost like they're being hypnotized by their hamsters."

"Are you thinking what I'm thinking?" I asked.

"But it can't be!" said Clementine. "According to the calendar, we still have sixteen days to go!"

"Have you ever thought that maybe your calendar idea could just be a great big bunch of doggy doo-doo?" I asked nicely.

"But Hot Dog isn't here!" Clementine continued. "Hot Dog *always* comes to help before the space aliens arrive!"

"Not this time," I said sadly. "This time it looks like it's just you and me!"

"Make that you and me and *them!*" Clementine shivered.

"Maybe we're overreacting," I said, turning my hamster upside down. "Maybe there's some perfectly logical explanation for what's going on here."

All of a sudden this funny kind of humming noise filled the room. At first it sounded like one little honeybee; then it got louder and louder and louder—until it sounded like a zillion quadrillion killer bees zooming in for the kill. Only we couldn't see any bees. We couldn't see anything unusual at all!

"This can*not* be good," Clementine said, shaking her head. "I mean it, Bob! This really can*not* be good!"

Chapter 5

Late Fees

"I don't get it," I said. "What's making that noise?"

"I never thought I'd say this," said Clementine, "but—*I want Hot Dog!!!*"

"Maybe something happened to him back on Dogzalot," I said. "Maybe the Big Bun took away his superhero privileges for messing up on too many missions or something."

"In that case," Clementine said, walking away, "how about *you* deal with this one by yourself? After all, you're Hot Dog's so-called *partner*. I'm just an innocent bystander!"

Right then the loud humming sound changed to an even louder WEEEEEEEE kind of noise.

"Look!" Clementine said, pointing at our classmates. "*They're* the ones making the noise! I think they're being controlled by these toys!"

"What's *WEEEEEEEE* supposed to mean?" I asked.

"I have no idea," said Clementine. "But I have a feeling we're going to find out."

I'd like to be able to tell you that Clementine was wrong. I'd like to be able to tell you that we never did find out what *WEEEEEEEE* meant. I'd like to be able to tell you that that was the end of all the weirdness forever and ever and that everything went back to normal just like in the good old days at Lugenheimer Elementary. But I can't.

"WEEEEEEEE," everyone chanted, staring blankly into the swirling eyes of the hamster toys. "WE ARE HAPPY HAMSTERS. WE LIKE TO RUN."

"I don't know about you," I said, heading for the door, "but I think I've had enough library time for today."

"I'm right behind you," Clementine said. "I'm sure not stickin' around to find out how *this* story ends!"

"I'd love to let you go. Really I would!" Miss Toenail said, blocking the door. "But until you

SKReeeeee

two return your overdue books, I'm afraid I can't let you leave this room."

Miss Toenail??? With all the weirdness, we'd completely forgotten about our friendly librarian.

"But we don't have any overdue books!" said Clementine.

"Of course you do!" Miss Toenail said, handing us a list of book titles.

Clementine read some of the titles out loud: "*How to Replace Electricity with Hamster Power; Good-Bye Gasoline, Hello Hamster Power; Reuse, Reduce, Rehamster; Human Beings Make Even Better Hamsters;* and *How to Hypnotize Humans So They Believe They're Hamsters and You Can Rule the World.*"

"But we never checked out any of these books!" I complained.

"Whoops! My mistake!" Miss Toenail said, ripping the list out of Clementine's hand. "*This* is your list of overdue library books!"

The list that Miss Toenail pulled out of her pocket was seriously at least a mile long.

"*The Complete Unabridged Encyclopaedia Britannica? Everything William Shakespeare Ever Wrote? The College Textbook of Psychology, Biology, and Every Other Ology Ever?* Um, I'm an okay reader," I said, "but this is ridiculous!"

"I can't possibly let you leave this library until all four million, eleven thousand and sixty-two books are returned," said Miss Toenail. "Either that or you can pay the late fees."

"I have a buck fifty!" I said, reaching into my pocket.

"Good for you!" said Miss Toenail. "Now all you need is another seventy gajillion dollars and eighty-four cents, and you're good to go!"

"WE ARE HAPPY HAMSTERS. WE LIKE TO RUN," chanted our spaced-out friends (and enemies, if you include Barfalot and his brainless bodyguards).

"That does it!" said Clementine. "I am definitely throwing away my calendar!"

Chapter 6

Bye-Bye, Miss Toenail; Hello, Hypnodini

Miss Toenail took out a big bag of sunflower seeds. "Who wants some yummy-nummy hamster treats?" she asked.

All the kids dropped their Hypnotic Hamster toys and ran to Miss Toenail with their tongues hanging out.

"Not so fast," she said. "Treat time comes after exercise time in this library!"

That's when things got extra-creepy.

A gigantic hamster wheel slowly rose up from the library floor.

"Hop on, my little pets!" Miss Toenail shouted. "A hamster's job is never done!"

Everybody hopped on the humongous wheel and ran.

"Don't stop running!" said Miss Toenail in a cheerful voice, with a smile on her face. "Never, ever stop running!"

The kids still looked like their regular old kid selves, only they really seemed to believe they were hamsters.

"WE ARE HAPPY HAMSTERS. WE LIKE TO RUN," they chanted as the wheel went around and around.

"You two, *too,* my precious little hamsters!" Miss Toenail said, shoving Clementine and me onto the wheel.

"But we're not hamsters!" Clementine yelled, shoving back.

"Of course you are, dear!" said Miss Toenail. "You are the first human hamsters to be part of my experiment here on your lovely little planet!"

42

"But you're our librarian!" said Clementine.

"No, I'm afraid your librarian had to go bye-bye," Miss Toenail said, peeling off her Miss Toenail mask and revealing a scary rodent monster face.

"I am the Amazing Hypnodini, hypnotizer of the universe! Once my new and improved Happy Hamster toys get out there, all the human beings on this planet will believe they're hamsters and will *live* to run on my

hamster wheels. Just imagine the power that will be generated by all those wheels going round and round, day and night, never, ever, *ever* stopping! Other planets will pay generously for my revolutionary new source of energy! Soon I shall be the richest hypnotizing genius in the universe! I tell you! Hamster power! Hamster power is the way!"

"Think again, Hypnodini!" Hot Dog said, zipping in through a crack in the library window.

"Hot Dog!" yelled Clementine. "What took you so long?"

"You'll never believe this," laughed Hot Dog. "The Big Bun beamed me into Bob's lunch box like usual, right? But get this! For some reason his lunch box was stuck under this giant bag of dog food underneath some leaky old sink! I thought I'd never get outta there!"

"Good one, Bob!" said Clementine.

Clementine was running behind me on the wheel so I couldn't see her face, but I could tell by her tone of voice that she was rolling her eyes at me.

Chapter 7

Prepare to Be Destroyed

"Shoo, fly!" Hypnodini said, picking up a fly swatter and swatting at Hot Dog. "Get away from my precious pets!"

"I ain't no fly, Hypnodini!" said Hot Dog. "And these kids here are people, not pets!"

"Oh, I beg to differ!" the alien said, stroking the ears of a Happy Hamster toy. "You hamsters have such nice hamster ears!"

All of a sudden *everyone* on the wheel had hamster ears. Next Hypnodini pulled on the toy's whiskers, saying, "And you hamsters have such nice hamster whiskers!" Then everyone had whiskers, too! Hypnodini was using the Happy Hamster toy like some kind of freaky control panel! Before we knew it, our classmates weren't just acting like hamsters; they were looking like them, too!

"Wait a minute; what's going on here?" growled Hypnodini. "Why aren't you two little pets turning into hamsters like the others?"

Clementine and I just looked at each other. This was our third alien attack, and for some reason we'd been immune to a bunch of the evil

magic every time. To be honest, we wanted to know what was up with that just as much as Hypnodini.

"Well, as long as you're askin'," said Hot Dog, "I'll tell ya. The almighty Big Bun on my peace-loving planet, Dogzalot, has provided my human partner and his helpful best friend here with a semiprotective coating."

"Semiprotective coating?" I said. "So *that's* what it is!"

"Not that I'm ungrateful or anything," Clementine said, running out of breath from running on the giant hamster wheel, "but as long as she was spraying it on, couldn't the Big Bun just as easily have gone with a hundred percent protective coating?"

"Full strength won't stick on humans," said Hot Dog. "Semiprotective is the best our scientists can do so far. But it's plenty strong to prevent somethin' as harmless as a little alien hypnotism."

"Impossible!" screeched Hypnodini. "No one is immune to the Amazing Hypnodini's hypnotic powers!"

The ugly rodent monster waved the Happy Hamster toy in front of us. Its crazy eyes turned from sunny yellow to bloody red. They spun around faster and faster and faster until— nothing! Nothing at all happened!

"Wow!" said Clementine. I guess that coating stuff really does work!"

"You have angered the Amazing Hypnodini!" screamed the weirdo. "I will destroy you unhypnotizable *dummy heads!* Prepare to be destroyed!"

Chapter 8

Hot Dog to the Rescue

"This is all your fault, Bob!" snarled Clementine. "If we ever get out of this library alive, will you kindly remind me not to ever be friends with you ever, ever, *ever* again?"

"This isn't my fault!" I argued. "How is it my fault? How come you always blame me for these alien invasions?"

"How come?" said Clementine. "How come? Well, how about for starters because *you're* the one who got picked to be Hot Dog's Earth partner!"

"And that's *my* fault exactly *how*?" I asked.

"And," Clementine continued, "how about because you gave me your stupid pencil when I forgot mine in Mrs. Itchybottom's first-grade class, basically forcing me to become your friend and stick by your side at terrible, life-threatening times like this!"

"Break it up, kiddos!" Hot Dog said, swooping down, his cape spreading out superhero style. "It wasn't an accident that the Big Bun picked you, partner. And you, little lady! If you think that the only reason you're always in on the alien-fighting game is your friend here, well, then, you'd better think again! And as far as you go, Miss Hypno-Whoever-You-Are, nobody calls my pals dummy heads! So if anybody's gonna be preparing to be destroyed, then it probably oughta be you!"

Hot Dog pushed one of his top-secret bun buttons and said, "Take that, baby!"

"Take what?" said Hypnodini.

"Hmm, the top-secret bun-button control panel must be jammed," Hot Dog said, trying all the buttons.

"Oh, silly me!" Clementine said. "I actually believed that your little super-dee-duper wannabe hero partner might actually make it through a whole mission without messing up *for once!* What in the world was I thinking?"

"Be quiet, Clem!" I whispered as I ran in place. "Hot Dog's bluffing! Those bun buttons never break. He's just playing with Hypnodini. You know, getting ready to make his move!"

Only I was wrong. It turned out that Hot Dog wasn't bluffing, playing, or making any moves. He was so busy trying to figure out what was jamming up his bun buttons he never even saw it coming. The little plastic hamster ball, that is. You know, the kind you can put your rodent in so it can run around the house without getting away?

"Run!" I yelled to Hot Dog. "You might be stuck in a ball, but you can still make a break for it! I've seen those things roll pretty fast. Just hurry up and get help!"

"Wait!" cried Clementine. "What's happening to him? Hot Dog! *Hot Dog*, are you okay?"

Hot Dog was gasping for air, opening and closing his tiny hot-doggy mouth like a fish out of water.

"Hot Dog!" I screamed, "you gotta tell me what to do!"

"There's nothing you *can* do," laughed Hypnodini. "There's nothing anyone can do! You want me to let you in on a little joke? That hamster ball has no airholes. Before long that annoying little pest will be gone for good!"

I watched helplessly as my limp little partner struggled to stay alive.

"I didn't mean that terrible thing I said about you, Hot Dog!" said Clementine. "It's not your fault that your bun buttons jammed up! I think you're a really good superhero! The best one I've ever met! Really, I do!"

Chapter 9

New Wallpaper

"No, *I'm* the one who's sorry!" Hot Dog gasped, bursting out of the ball. "Sorry it took me so long to remember that the Dogzalot technology team recently installed this handy-dandy new reset button for situations just like this one!"

The plastic hamster ball shattered into a million pieces, and Hot Dog pushed a bun button, squirting ketchup all over Hypnodini.

"AARRGGHH! EWWW!" hollered Hypnodini.

Hot Dog pushed another button, and pickle relish blopped out all over Hypnodini.

"GRODY! SICKY! YUCK!" hollered Hypnodini.

Then Hot Dog pushed another button, and bun crumbs blasted out all over Hypnodini.

"BLECHH! OOCKY!" hollered Hypnodini.

"What's happening to her?" asked Clementine. "She's swelling up! She's getting enormous!"

"Like one of those giant Thanksgiving Day Parade balloons you see on TV," I agreed, "only covered in foody grossness."

"I've said it before, and I'll say it again,"
Hot Dog said, rubbing his little hot-doggy
hands together proudly. "Bun crumbs and evil
simply do not mix!"

"I'll get you, you weird weenie!" moaned
Hypnodini. "Nobody tangles with the hamster-
power queen of the universe!"

Hypnodini was definitely having some kind of nasty allergic reaction to the bun crumbs or something because she was still inflating—getting bigger and bigger and—

"Better get ready, kids," Hot Dog said, leaping behind a bookshelf. "This is gonna be a messy one!"

Clementine and I jumped off the hamster wheel and ducked underneath the computer table.

KERPLOWY! The huge, hamstery balloon popped—all over the place!

"Lovely!" gagged Clementine. "Our school library has new wallpaper!"

"Well, so much for anybody gettin' rich off hamster power!" said Hot Dog. "Now all we need to do is get this place cleaned up, and I'm outta here!"

"Wait! What about *them?*" I said, pointing up at our hamster-people classmates, who were still running in place zombie style on the huge hamster wheel.

"Hmm, they're still hamsters?" said Hot Dog. "That's funny!"

Funny? Funny wasn't exactly the word I had in mind. The word I had in mind was more like *terrible!* or *freaky!* or possibly even *disastrous!* Why was that huge hamster wheel still in the library? Why were our classmates still hamster people? And now that Hypnodini was out of the picture, who would *un*hypnotize them? Wasn't it supposed to go back to normal once the big bad alien was gone? Why, oh why wasn't everything going back to normal?

"This cannot be good," said Clementine. "This really can*not* be good!"

Chapter 9½

Can You Relate?

Have you ever had a bad day? No, I mean a really *bad* day! You know, the kind where even the pitiful life of a partly squished banana slug seems better than yours. And then, have you ever had that bad day get better? And you start to think that maybe your life might be worth living after all? And then, just when you're scraping your sad little self up off the ground, ready to give life another chance—WHAM!!! Everything gets even worse than before?

If you answered yes, then maybe, just maybe, you can relate to how I was feeling that day.

The Experiment

"No problem," said Hot Dog. "Your classmates only look like hamsters because they really believe they're hamsters. All we have to do is snap them out of Hypnodini's evil trance, and they'll go back to normal."

"And we do this unhypnotizing thing exactly *how?*" asked Clementine.

"See the little knob right here on the back of all the Happy Hamster toys?" said Hot Dog.

Clementine and I looked clueless and surprised at the same time.

"How'd we miss those?" asked Clementine.

"Sometimes it takes a superhero to notice the details," said Hot Dog. "Anywho, if I'm guessin' right, all we gotta do is give this little knob the old twisteroo, and—presto change-o— your classmates here'll be back to normal!"

"Look!" I said. "Turning that knob made its eyes spin in the opposite direction!"

"You better believe it, partner!" said Hot Dog.
"And now, if you'll help me turn all these knobs
and get all these unhypnotizing Happy Hamster
toys passed out, maybe I'll make it back to
Dogzalot in time to watch the game with my
buddies after all."

"Hold on a minute!"
I thought to myself. "Hot Dog
has buddies? Are *they*
superhero hot dogs, too? And
they sit around watching games
together? Just like we do here on Earth? What
kinds of games do they play on Dogzalot?"
I was dying to find out the answers, but I was
even more curious to find out if Hot Dog's idea
was going to work.

We turned the knobs on all the toys and handed them out to the super-tired hamster people. The first part of the experiment went okay. Our classmates stared straight into those crazy swirly Happy Hamster eyes, no problem. But the second part—well, that, unfortunately, didn't exactly go according to plan.

It turned out that instead of reversing Hypnodini's hypnotic spell, turning the knob on the Happy Hamster toys only made our friends run backward!

"Hmm, that's funny!" said Hot Dog.

Once again, *funny* wasn't even close to any of the words I was thinking of. The words I was

thinking of were more like *lousy excuse for a superhero.* I know that's not very nice. And I know none of this was really Hot Dog's fault. But when your superhero partner makes everything worse instead of better, it can be kind of annoying. Plus, you know how the reverse knob made the Happy Hamsters' eyes spin backward? Well, that's not all it did to them.

Psycho Hypno Hamsters

I guess you could say the Happy Hamster toys didn't look too happy anymore. Their eyebrows switched from cute and friendly to mean and bushy. Their fuzzy feet sprouted scratchy claws. Their friendly mouths sprouted unfriendly fangs. They scrambled all over the library.

They were alive and they were *everywhere!* They were hanging from the ceiling. They were climbing on the bookshelves, and before we knew it, the psycho hypno hamsters had all three of us surrounded. Then, just when things couldn't possibly get any worse—they got worse!

Chapter 11

Teamwork

Two of the freaky hamster-toy guys squeaked, "*Yee-haw!*" and threw this strange whiskery rope around us like they were cowboys showing off their lasso tricks. And just like that, Hot Dog, Clementine and I were hog-tied like three little piggies at a rodeo.

"Do something!" I yelled at Hot Dog.

"I'm tryin'!" yelled Hot Dog. "But I can't reach it!"

"Reach what?" Clementine yelled as the psycho zombie hamster mob moved in closer and closer.

"If I could just push my blue bun button," Hot Dog grunted, "then I could—"

Those bun buttons had saved us before, and as long as that control panel wasn't jammed again—I didn't even wait to hear the end of Hot Dog's sentence.

"Are you thinking what I'm thinking?" I asked Clementine.

"Use that!" Clementine said, spotting a nearby pencil. "I'll scoot it toward you, and you grab it with your teeth!"

The three of us were the perfect team. Clementine scooted, I grabbed, and Hot Dog wiggled till his bun was within reach. I'd never actually seen all those eensy-weensy bun buttons up close. I thought he had five or six— maybe seven—of the things. But there were a bunch of them!

I panicked. What if I pushed the wrong one? What if I made things even worse? The Big Bun would never forgive me. And who knew what she'd do to Hot Dog if he failed on this mission? From what I'd heard, the last thing you ever want to do is bum out the almighty ruler of Dogzalot. My heart was racing. My face was dripping sweat.

"Bob!" yelled Clementine. "Hurry up and push it already!"

I gripped the pencil between my tightly clenched teeth. I lined up the pointy lead with the microscopic blue button, and I pushed.

Chapter 12

Blue Stuff

A powerful blue spray shot out of Hot Dog's bun like water exploding from a fire hydrant and filled the air with a thick blue fog. For a minute I couldn't see anything but blue. And in that minute, although I could barely see, I breathed a sigh of relief. Those out-of-control zombie-eyed hypno hamsters had disappeared from Lugenheimer Elementary's library faster than extra-double-frosted cupcakes from a tray at a birthday party.

I could tell because the unexplainable smell I always smelled whenever evil aliens were around was completely gone. Plus, the pitiful panting noises that my hamsterized class-mates had been making on the giant wheel had changed to the regular sounds of regular people just talking regularly.

"Hot Dog! You did it!" said Clementine. "The Happy Hamsters are gone, and the kids are kids again!"

"Correction, my friend," said Hot Dog. "*We* did it!"

I had to admit that the three of us did make a pretty good team. And I don't know what was in that blue stuff, but it sure worked. The library and everyone in it were back to normal. (A little blue, but back to normal.) Even the Hypnodini wallpaper was totally gone.

Hot Dog dusted himself off and pushed his famous make-everyone-forget-that-evil-aliens-or-flying weenies-were-ever-here button. And just like on his last two missions, a cool, sparkly shower of forgetting mist swirled around the room.

"Five minutes till kickoff!" he said, shaking our hands. "It looks like I'm gonna be able to watch that game with my buddies after all!"

The little guy smoothed out his cape, waved good-bye and flew out the same crack in the library window that he'd flown in through.

Chapter 13

Time Warp

I waved back at Hot Dog and blinked to get the forgetting mist out of my eyes. But when I opened them up again, it was like time had rewound back to when this whole hamster disaster first started.

"So, here y'all go. There's a Happy Hamster in this here box for each and every one of y'all!" Angelina's mother said cheerfully.

"Huh?" said Clementine, "Didn't we already do this?"

"I don't get it," I said. "There is *no way* I can handle a repeat of this day!"

But luckily this time was different. This time the box didn't say "Rejects." This time the only ones shoving and grabbing were Barfalot and his brainless bodyguards. This time Angelina's mother just handed each of us a cheapo-looking hamster toy that wasn't much more interesting than the dental floss we got from Marco's dad

the dentist. And this time Miss Toenail was too busy trying to figure out why little bits of blue were all over the place to worry about telling us to be quiet.

"Man! My legs are killing me!" Marco said on our way out of the library. "Why do I feel like I totally just ran a marathon?"

"Believe me," I said, "you really do *not* want to know!"

"Sure I do!" Marco said, tossing his Happy Hamster up in the air. "What's goin' on?"

"I thought Career Day was just fascinating!" Clementine said, switching the subject. "Didn't you guys think Career Day was just fascinating?"

"Oh, yeah! Career Day was just fascinating!" I agreed. "Too bad it's over!"

"I know," said Clementine. "I am seriously bummed that it's over!"

"You guys are so *different!*" laughed Marco.

"Marco," said Clementine, "you have *no* idea!"

(for now)

As an award-winning investigative reporter specializing in extraterrestrial activity, **L. Bob Rovetch** has spent hundreds of hours interviewing Bob and helping him record his amazing but true adventures. Ms. Rovetch lives across the Golden Gate Bridge from San Francisco with two perfect children and plenty of pets.

Dave Whamond wanted to be a cartoonist ever since he could pick up a crayon. During math classes he would doodle in the margin of his papers. One math teacher warned him, "You'd better spend more time on your math and less time cartooning. You can't make a living drawing funny pictures." Today Dave has a syndicated daily comic strip, called *Reality Check.* Dave has one wife, two kids, one dog and one kidney. They all live together in Calgary, Alberta.

Look out!
The Dogwash Doggies Are
Coming Your Way!

Just when you thought the world was safe! Arriving in Fall 2007:

Hot Dog and Bob and the Surprisingly Slobbery Attack of the Dogwash Doggies

The adventures of Hot Dog and Bob continue in this bone-chewing new episode! All is going well at the fifth-grade fundraiser until talking dogs from the planet Bowwowwowwow, arrive to take over Earth and turn Bob and his unsuspecting classmates into their pets! Hot Dog and Bob must battle this new lazer-beam-chewie-wielding alien duo to save the world!